MASTER
OF MY
UNIVERSE

Explore the universe in search of new worlds.
Your story has 8 episodes. Each episode has
missions you must complete to be the master
of your universe. Go boldly, go bravely,
go where no one has gone before!

make
believe
ideas

EPISODE 1 - DISCOVERY

Complete every episode in this book and you will be:

MASTER OF YOUR UNIVERSE.

But first you need a planet and you need to travel there. Look at the screen.
There are dangers in your path – mark each one with an X on the grid opposite.
When you have plotted all the obstacles, start from the red triangle at J8
and find the shortest route to the planet at A7 without hitting anything!

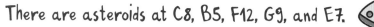

There are satellites at H3, D3, H4, I10, and D11.

There are asteroids at C8, B5, F12, G9, and E7.

There is toxic space junk at H7, H8, E10, F13, and C5.

There are comets at D10, B13, F3, and B3.

There are hostile alien ships at D12, B6, and D5.

There are stars at D15, G7, F14, and F4.

There are black holes at C6, F5, F8, and C10.

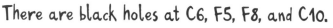

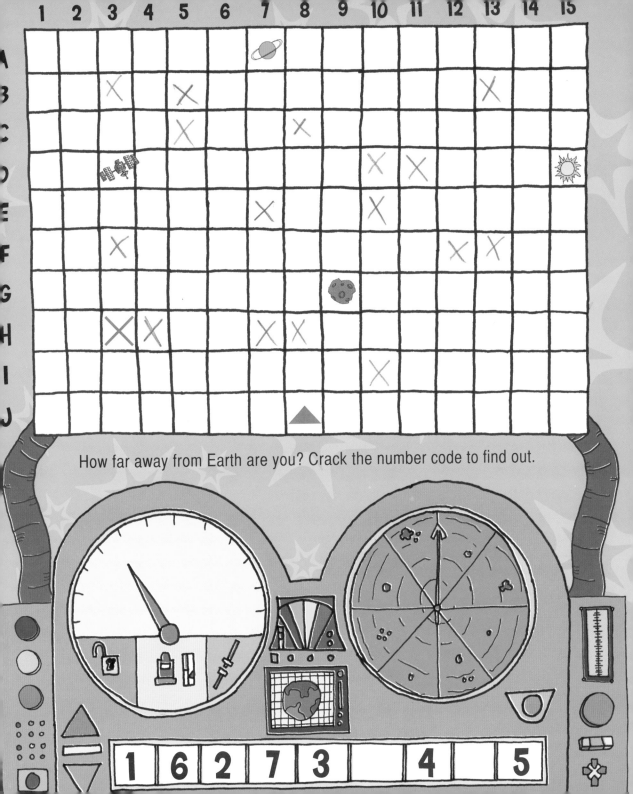

How far away from Earth are you? Crack the number code to find out.

THIS IS YOUR UNIVERSE

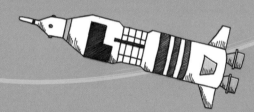

Write your full name here, then use the letters to complete the planets' names. You can use the letters as many times as you like.

Alekzander ☐☐☐☐☐☐☐☐☐☐☐☐☐☐☐☐☐
☐☐☐☐☐☐☐☐☐☐☐☐☐☐☐☐☐☐☐☐☐☐☐☐☐☐☐

Here it is – IT'S ALL YOURS!

Write your planet's name in the banner, then fill it with seas, deserts, and mountains.

game planet

Time for a bit of **INVESTIGATION.**

our craft has the technology to study your planet even before you land.
dd arrows to the dials and shade the gauges to record your findings.

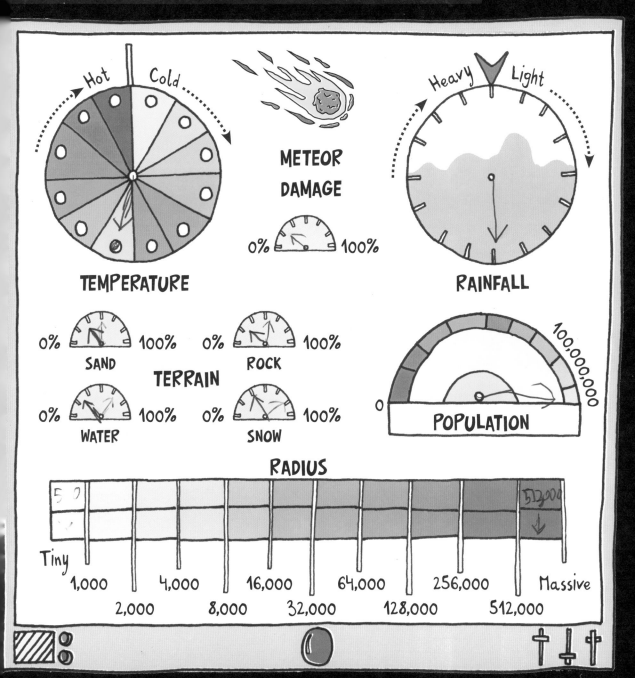

TEMPERATURE

Hot   Cold

METEOR DAMAGE

0%   100%

RAINFALL

Heavy   Light

0% SAND 100%   0% ROCK 100%

TERRAIN

0% WATER 100%   0% SNOW 100%

0   POPULATION   100,000,000

RADIUS

Tiny

1,000   4,000   16,000   64,000   256,000   Massive

2,000   8,000   32,000   128,000   512,000

512000

Your land needs a
CAPITAL CITY.
Make yours AWESOME!

Build more towers, then go underground.
Take the tunnel to Episode 2.
Don't bump into any bones!

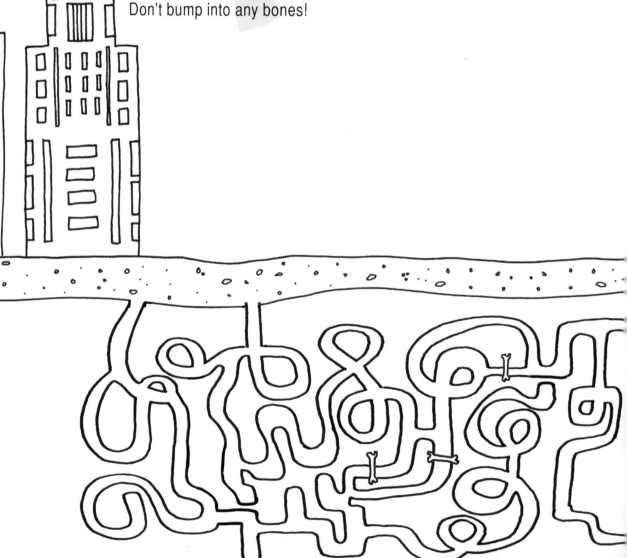

EPISODE 2 – GROUND CONTROL

One great thing about being in charge of everything is that you can live wherever you want and build your own HQ, or control center.

WE GIVE YOU A DOOR.
WE GIVE YOU A ROOF.
DESIGN THE REST.

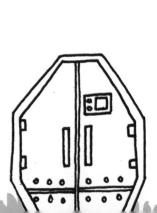

Things are looking good in your universe.

THE NEXT THING YOU NEED IS YOUR OWN PERSONAL FLAG SO **EVERYONE** KNOWS WHO IS **BOSS**. DESIGN IT HERE.

Here's how your
HQ IS LAID OUT.

Use the checklist to decide what rooms you need and then come up with some of your own. Plot your rooms and any special features on the floor plans.

- [ ] Theater room
- [ ] Indoor pool
- [ ] Kitchen
- [ ] Gym
- [ ] Game room
- [ ] Bathroom
- [ ] Bedroom
- [ ] Bowling alley
- [ ] Dance floor
- [ ] Study
- [ ] Indoor football field
- [ ] ....
- [ ] ....
- [ ] ....
- [ ] ....

LEVEL 1

LEVEL 2

LEVEL 3

Not many people appreciate just how tiring being Top Dog can be. You really are out there ruling 24/7/365, so you need to have all the latest comforts and conveniences, such as this Ultimate Snax vending machine.

Fill it with whatever you like.

This chair is **THE BOSS OF CHAIRS.**

It's practically your **THRONE.**

Decide what it does and give it extra parts if you want.

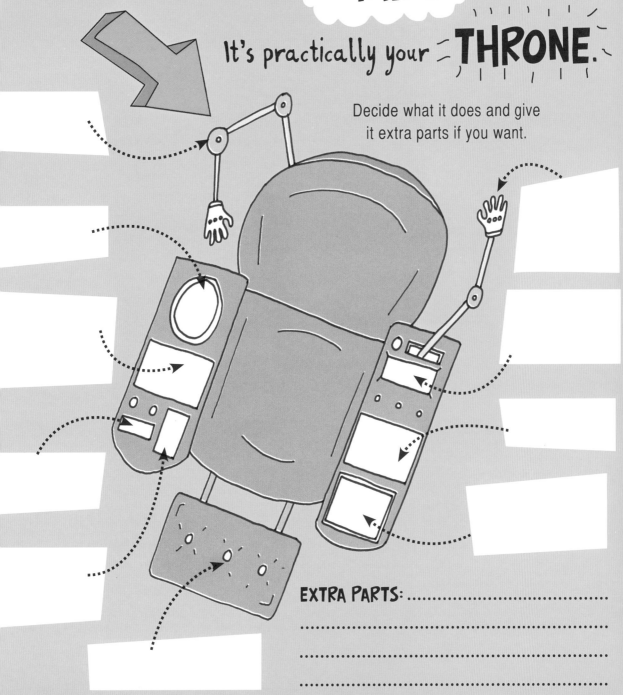

EXTRA PARTS: ....

....

....

....

You need gadgets to help you
RULE THE UNIVERSE!

Here's your phone. **IT'S AWESOME.**

Decide on its functions and fill the screen.

FUNCTIONS:

....

....

....

MOMU

Fill in your watch face.

IS IT JUST A WATCH?

You decide.

FUNCTIONS:

....

....

....

This mega-bed has four robotic arms.

Decide what the arms control.

Sleep well, you have work to do...

Create your own CURRENCY!

To get your planet really moving
and shaking, you'll need your own money.

In the box below are names of seven Earth currencies. Draw two lines between the letters to create the name of your currency. For example, you could call your currency the "Larpo."

DOLLARPOUNDPESORUPEEYENEURORUBL

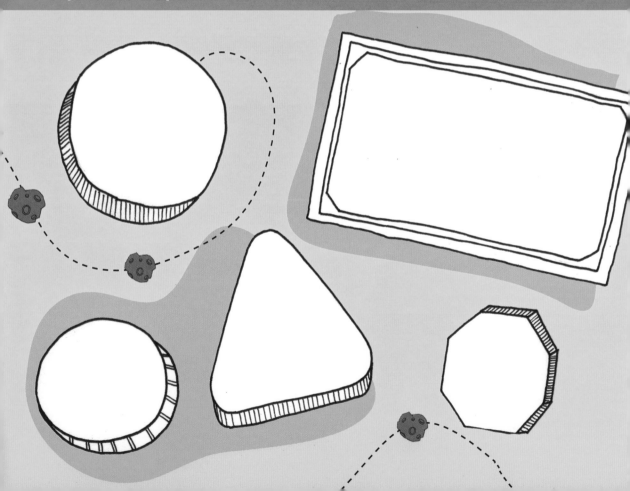

...hink of some items and write their prices in your new currency.

ITEM	PRICE

EPISODE 3 – INVENT A LANGUAGE

You can speak English in your universe, but it would be way more cool to have your own secret code or language. Here are three ways to make a code or a language.

1. First, find your birthday number. Take the date of your birthday and add all the numbers together. For example, if your birthday is 12/03/2003, your number is 11 (1+2+3+2+3). (If your number is 26, take away 3.) Starting at the star, move 11 spaces clockwise. On the eleventh space write the letter A under the L. Continue writing the rest of the alphabet around the wheel. Use the wheel to translate words. In this example Mars becomes Bpgh!

2. Use your birthday number to transform a word by switching the vowels (A, E, I, O, U). (If your birthday number ends in 5 or 0, take away 2.) Then, starting at the star, count clockwise around the light blue spaces on the inner circle. Where you stop write A, then fill in the rest of the vowels in order, E – I – O – U, in the other four light blue boxes. Use this to translate words by swapping the vowels. So, in this example, Mars would become Murs.

3. Change the sound and look of a word by adding extra letters. Pick one of the four letter combinations in the green center and add it after the first vowel (A, E, I, O, U) in the word. So, if you picked "BU," Mars would become Maburs.

Give your language a name...

Translate these words...

ROCKET	
SPACE	
ALIEN	
HELLO	
AWESOME	

EPISODE 4 – LAW AND ORDER

uling your own planet can take up a lot of time, so it's a good idea to have people
do stuff for you. Choose four Chief jobs from the list. Appoint your friends to the jobs
nd cartoon their portraits in the frames.

Chief of:

Chief of:

Chief of:

Chief of:

CHIEF OF...

Smart Stuff

Sport

Snacks

Back-chat

Dumb Stuff

Gross Stuff

Technology

Chore Avoidance

Comedy

Games

IT'S THE LAW!

The best thing about running the show is that you make the rules. Write down some new laws to suit you.

It is the law that everyone in my land must . . .

1. ....
2. ....
3. ....
4. ....

And that everyone must not . . .

1. ....
2. ....
3. ....
4. ....

On NO ACCOUNT may old people (especially parents) do the following . . .

1. ....
2. ....
3. ....
4. ....

These things are absolutely banned in my land . . .

1. ....
2. ....
3. ....
4. ....

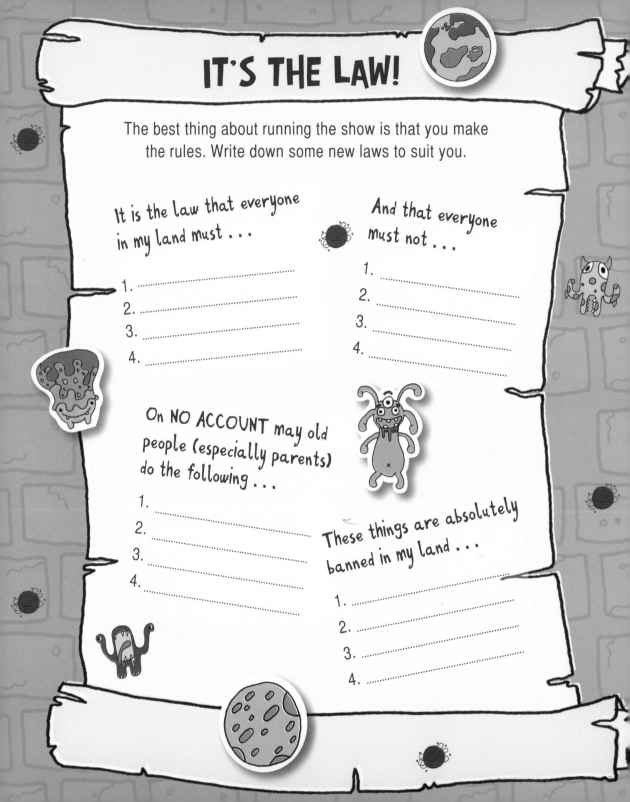

Sadly, even on the happiest of planets,
RULES WILL BE BROKEN.

Think of suitable punishments for rule breakers! Look at the first ball and chain, then close your eyes and let the tip of your finger fall down onto the ball. Write down the word nearest to your finger. Do this with the other two balls so you have three words. Now, put them into a sentence describing the punishment, then make up another.

Poke
Eat
Trap
Squeeze
Wear
Lick

Cold
Toe
Fish
Sock
Underpants
Sandwich
Worm
Finger

Week
Hour
Day
Year
Night

1.	2.	3.

PUNISHMENT: ....

1.	2.	3.

PUNISHMENT: ....

SPACE COP!

Draw the other half of the space cop. Will he be the same? Will his other half be completely different?

YOUR PLANET, you decide!

EPISODE 5 – RELAX, YOU RULE

Phew! After all that serious being-in-charge stuff, you'll need some serious relaxation time.

INVENT A NEW SPORT FOR YOUR PLANET HERE.

Soccer

Tennis

Golf

Football

Squash

Baseball

Mash up any sport from the left with any sport from the right and write the new name below, for example: Squash + Sumo = Squmo

+

=

Wrestling

Cycling

Bowling

Hockey

Sumo

RULES OF THE GAME: ....

....

....

....

THE NEW SPORT OF:

Pokmon

Any self-respecting, intergalactic sports team needs cool shoes and uniforms. Design them here, then design the championship cup.

Be a sporting legend!

pokemon

Invent four perfect TV channels, then name them and draw their logos here.

What kind of spaceships do you see at Christmas?

U F HO, HO, HOs!

Why did the aliens leave the moon party?

Because there was no atmosphere!

Why did the space cow make a detour?

Because she heard it was the Milky Way!

A GALAXY OF GAGS

What music do planets dance to?

Nep-tunes!

Why did the star leave school?

He thought he was bright enough!

Why don't stars read novels?

Because they prefer comet books!

These jokes are out of this world! Give each one a planet rating out of 5.

What do you call an alien with no eyes?

Alen!

Where does Buzz Lightyear keep his snacks?

In his launch box!

Why did the cow become an astronaut?

Because she wanted to see the mooooooooooon!

When does the moon burp?

When it's full!

What did Mars say to Saturn when they met at a party?

Give me a ring sometime!

What do you call a three-eyed alien?

Aliiien!

ALIEN AMBUSH!

Stare at the screen for 10 seconds, then hold a pencil with its point touching the start star. Now close your eyes tightly and attempt to draw a path to the finish star without running into the aliens! Start with 100 points and lose 20 points for every alien you run over.

START!

SCORE:

FINISH!

EPISODE 6 - ASTROCRAFT

When you're king of the world, it's important to have your own custom-made transportation. Begin with a fleet of super spacecraft. Design the tail fins and add the windows and side decals.

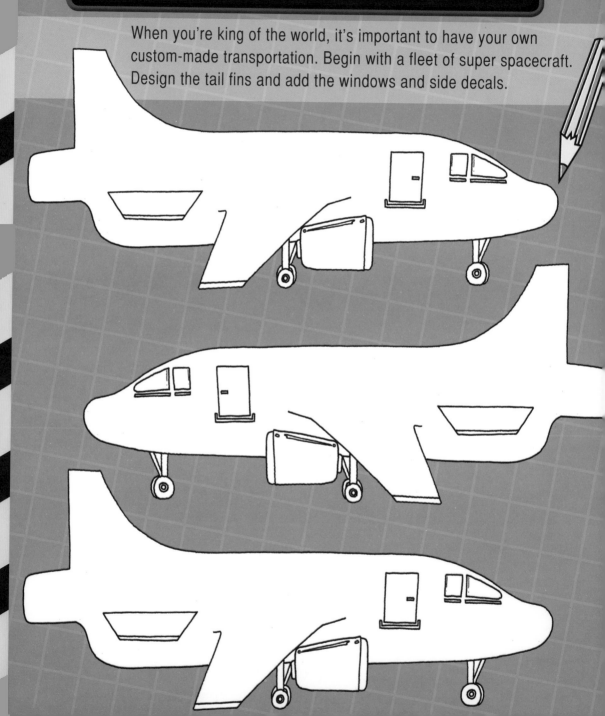

RAGING ROCKETS

There are over 200 rockets on this
page, but only one that's different.
You have 30 seconds to find it.
Then turn the page.

COOL CARS

Create your fleet of cool custom cars, then fill in the specs below.

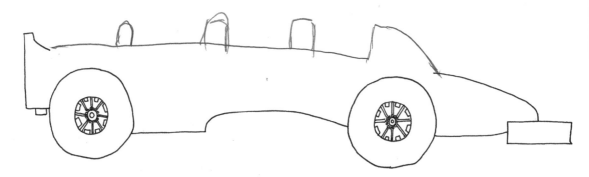

Length 7   Height 14   Seats 29   Top speed 1,00000 hp   Special feature Stickers

Length ___   Height ___   Seats ___   Top speed _____   Special feature _____

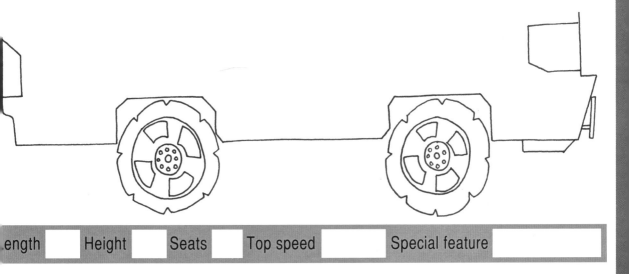

Length [ ]　Height [ ]　Seats [ ]　Top speed [ ]　Special feature [ ]

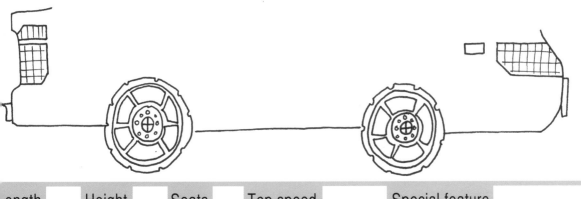

Length [ ]　Height [ ]　Seats [ ]　Top speed [ ]　Special feature [ ]

MOTOR MASH-UP

In outer space things can get weird.
Imagine a mash-up of two totally
different types of transportation,
then design it in the grids.

Pickup

Bus

Monster Truck + Helicopter

Submarine

SUV

+

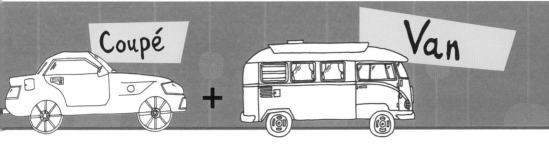

Coupé

Van

+

EPISODE 7 – INTERGALACTIC EXPLORATION

Now that you're settled on your planet, it's time to explore some more of the universe. Good thing you've got a space station – here it is!

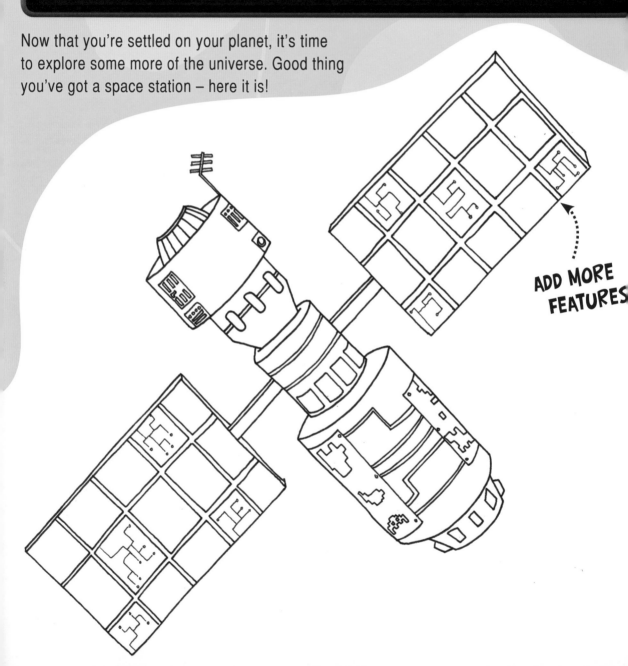

ADD MORE FEATURES

ick a planet from your universe and write its name in the sign.

Draw its **four** most interesting features.

EXPLORE THE PLANET

Take time to look around. Draw what you see.

ALIENS!

Whoa! The thing about intergalactic space travel is that you never know who or what you might find. Complete the drawings of these awesome creatures.

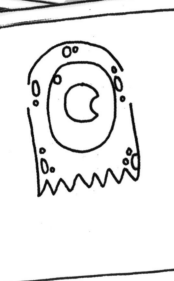

Astro Clive

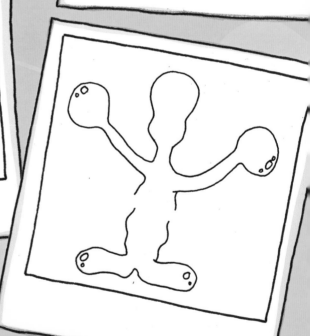

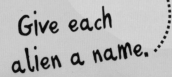

Give each alien a name.

What else did you find?

GREEN ALIENS

The aliens' Transform-a-rator turns space junk into totally awesome transporters. Transform the trash into alien cars, boats, and planes.

Umbrella boat

EXPLORATION REPORT

Enter your home planet's name at the top of the left screen and the name of the planet you are exploring at the top of the right screen. Fill in the data fields, then compare planets.

PLANET NAME:
....

CAPITAL CITY:
....

CURRENCY:

NATIONAL ANTHEM (pick a song):
....

PLANTS:

Biggest	Smallest	Most awesome

AGE OF PLANET (YRS):
....

SIZE OF POPULATION:

OLDEST INHABITANT (YRS):
....

LIVES MAINLY:
○ in the city
○ in the country
○ underwater
○ in the sky

TRAVELS MAINLY:
○ on water
○ on land
○ in the air
○ underground

CLIMATE:
Cold ● ● ● ● ● ● ● Hot
Wet ● ● ● ● ● ● ● Dry

OTHER LIFE-FORMS:..
....

TERRAIN: ○ Flat ○ Hilly ○ Desert ○ Rain forest ○ Mountains ○ Ice & snow

INHABITANTS' SUPER-HUMAN POWERS:

○ Invisibility
◉ Mega-speed
○ Transformation powers
○ Mind-reading

○ Extra limbs
○ Size-changing
◉ Never sleeping
○ Mega-memory

○ Flying
◉ Mega-strength
○ Stretchy body
○ Breathing underwater

PLANET NAME:

....

NAME OF CAPITAL CITY: ....

CURRENCY:

....

NATIONAL ANTHEM (pick a song):

....

PLANTS:

Biggest	Smallest	Most awesome

AGE OF PLANET (YRS):

SIZE OF POPULATION:

OLDEST INHABITANT (YRS):

LIVES MAINLY:
- ◯ in the city
- ◯ in the country
- ◯ underwater
- ◯ in the sky

TRAVELS MAINLY:
- ◯ on water
- ◯ on land
- ◯ in the air
- ◯ underground

CLIMATE:

Cold ● ● ● ● ● ● ● Hot

Wet ● ● ● ● ● ● ● Dry

OTHER LIFE-FORMS: ....

....

TERRAIN: ◯ Flat ◯ Hilly ◯ Desert ◯ Rain forest ◯ Mountains ◯ Ice & snow

INHABITANTS' SUPER-HUMAN POWERS:

- ◯ Invisibility
- ◉ Mega-speed
- ◯ Transformation powers
- ◯ Mind-reading

- ◯ Extra limbs
- ◯ Size-changing
- ◉ Never sleeping
- ◯ Mega-memory

- ◯ Flying
- ◯ Mega-strength
- ◯ Stretchy body
- ◉ Breathing underwater

It's nearly time for the ultimate space adventure. You will shortly undertake the biggest challenge of your amazing voyage.

First you must unlock the secret password, which will grant you entry into the final episode.

Locate these words in the data grid. When you find them, shade them in. The shaded boxes will reveal the password.

TIME SOLAR
ROCKET PODS
PLANET
NANO ATE
MARTIAN
METAL
ANTS
ARM MOON
METEORS SOS

★	Z	E	H	V	W	A	I	O	H	Y	P
C	M	O	O	N	R	K	Y	S	O	T	S
J	A	Y	N	Q	Z	G	B	P	F	Y	O
H	R	O	C	M	J	E	C	🪐	G	I	R
P	T	I	M	E	O	F	K	C	Y	X	G
G	I	Q	D	W	K	B	U	Y	M	N	D
N	A	Y	M	N	K	H	R	Q	A	K	N
I	N	A	N	O	N	C	S	I	U	J	M
G	V	W	Q	I	G	P	W	Y	V	K	G
E	S	O	Y	F	D	N	P	O	D	S	K
D	A	Z	S	D	L	B	L	R	H	O	D
R	I	N	E	🌑	O	A	A	N	T	S	N
C	P	U	B	S	M	Q	N	U	A	L	H
E	Y	T	J	R	L	V	E	P	S	D	F
F	S	N	Y	B	T	X	T	F	L	W	J
L	W	A	Z	E	M	U	Y	J	R	E
K	M	U	T	F	X	B	V	S	B	U	T
V	C	W	R	P	S	J	🪐	N	Z	W	C
H	L	K	F	Y	T	K	A	S	Q	V	G
X	☀	Q	G	K	D	B	B	V	N	Q	J

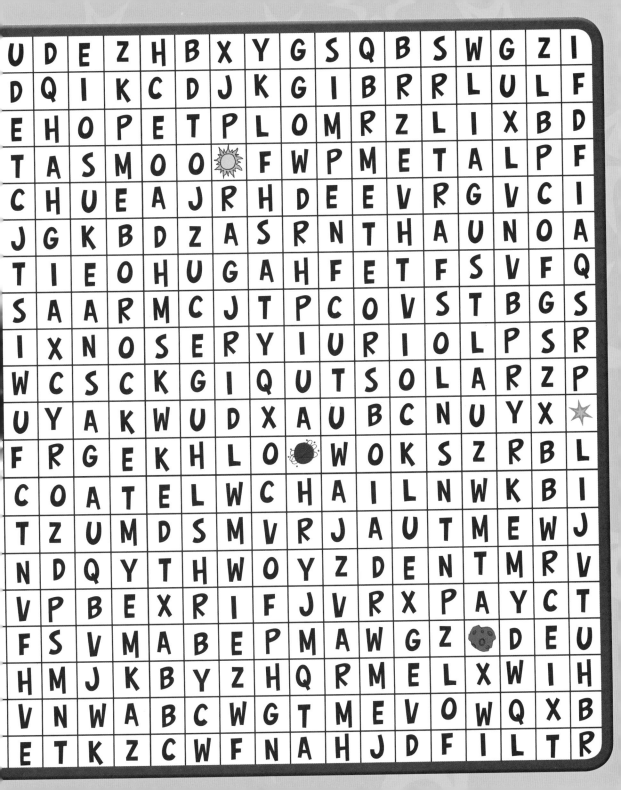

EPISODE 8 - ALIEN ENCOUNTER

Now it's time for you to take total control. Pick up the story. Having established your own planet, your intergalactic exploration has also led to the discovery of a new world. Do the people live in peace? Do they wage war? Do they work together to discover new planets? How does the environment, terrain, and technology affect the story? Do you ever go back to your own planet?

OVER TO YOU . . .

Plan your adventure and practice your cartooning here.

ALIEN
ENCOUNTER

An intergalactic adventure by:

Alek

PART 1. IN WHICH THE EPIC ADVENTURE BEGINS.

PART 2. IN WHICH...

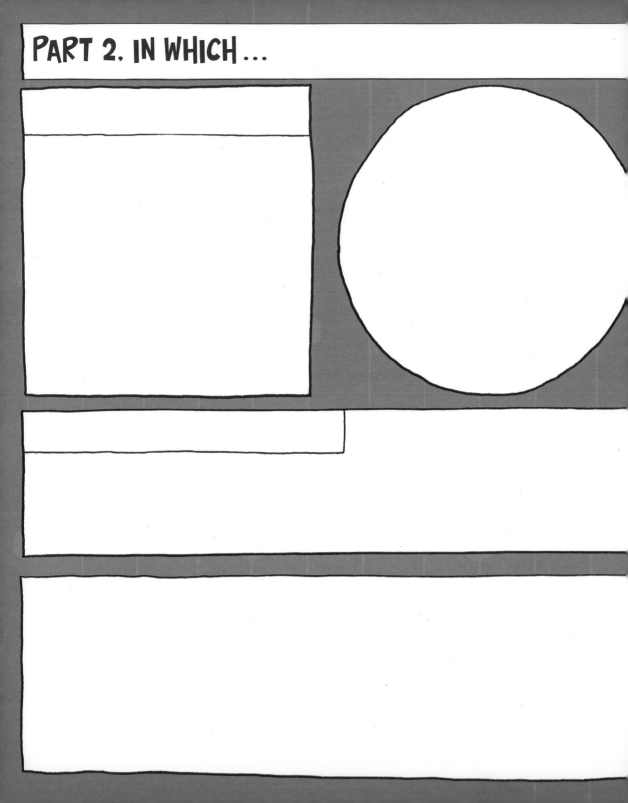

PART 3. IN WHICH ...

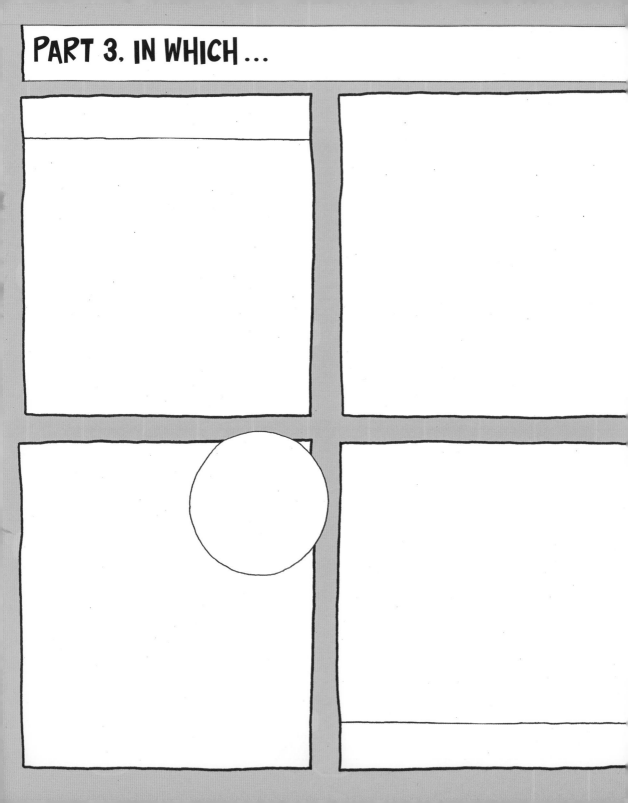

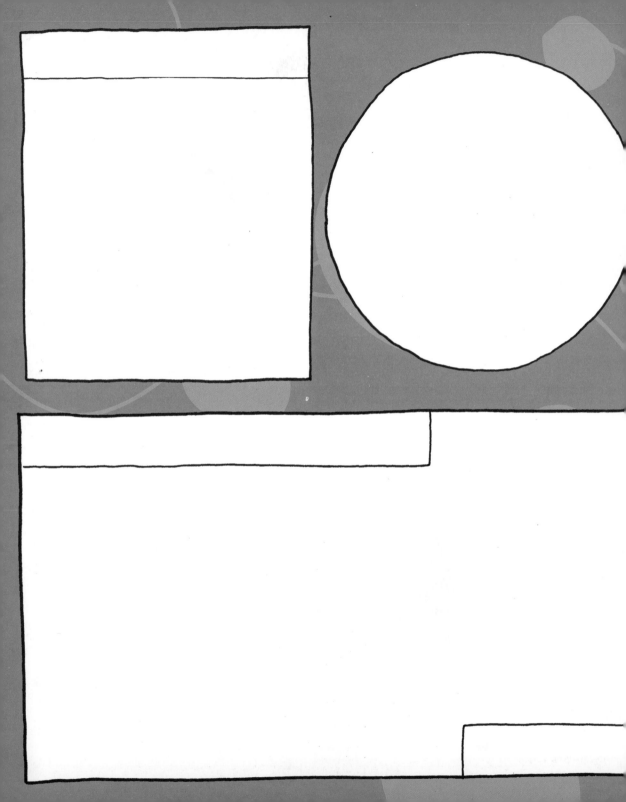